This book belongs to:

_____

To Valentine, the horse,
Edward, the donkey,
Ted, the dog,
and our cat, Tex

This paperback edition published in 2011 by Andersen Press L
Published in Australia by Random House Australia Pty., Leve
100 Pacific Highway, North Sydney, NSW 20
First published in Great Britain in 2003 by Andersen Press L
Text and illustration copyright © Michael Foreman, 20
The rights of Michael Foreman to be identified as the author and illustra
of this work have been asserted by them in accordance with
Copyright, Designs and Patents Act, 1988. All rights reserv
Colour separated in Switzerland by Photolitho AG, Züri
Printed and bound in Singapore by Tien Wah Pr
Michael Foreman has used watercolour in this bo
10   9   8   7   6   5   4   3   2
British Library Cataloguing in Publication Data available. ISBN 978 1 84270 47

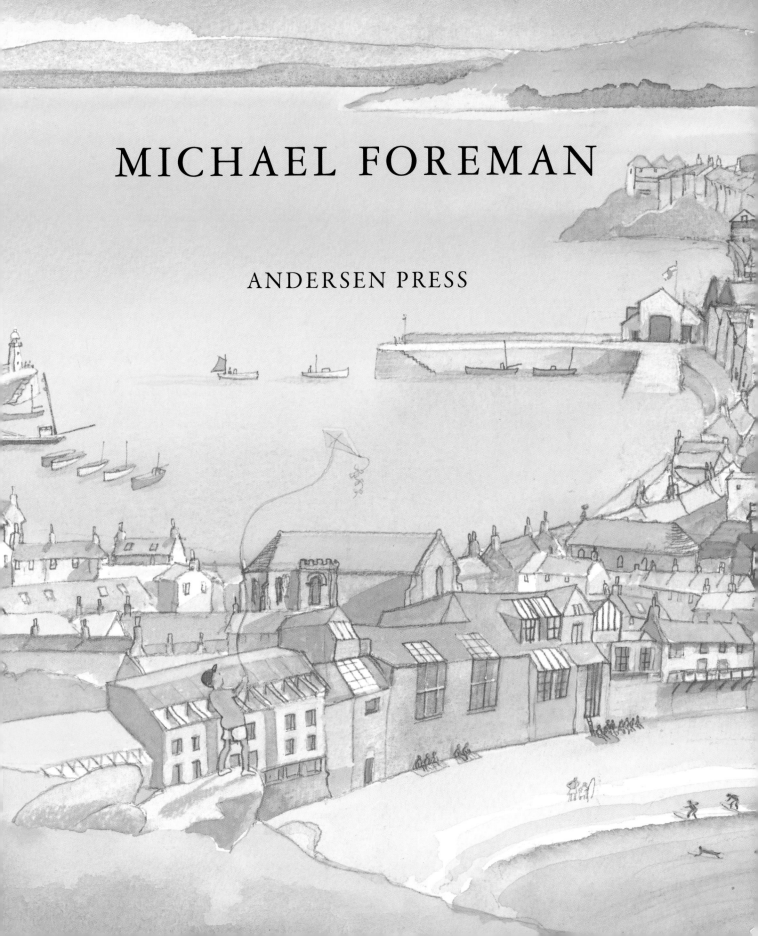

# CAT on the HILL

MICHAEL FOREMAN

ANDERSEN PRESS

# SUMMER

AAAH! It's good to be here, under these old stone steps. And just look at that view! No wonder people climb up here every day just to have a look. Nice people, too. They share their picnics with me, especially the children. They feed me bits from their sandwiches and drips from their ice-creams. Chocolate ripple is my favourite.

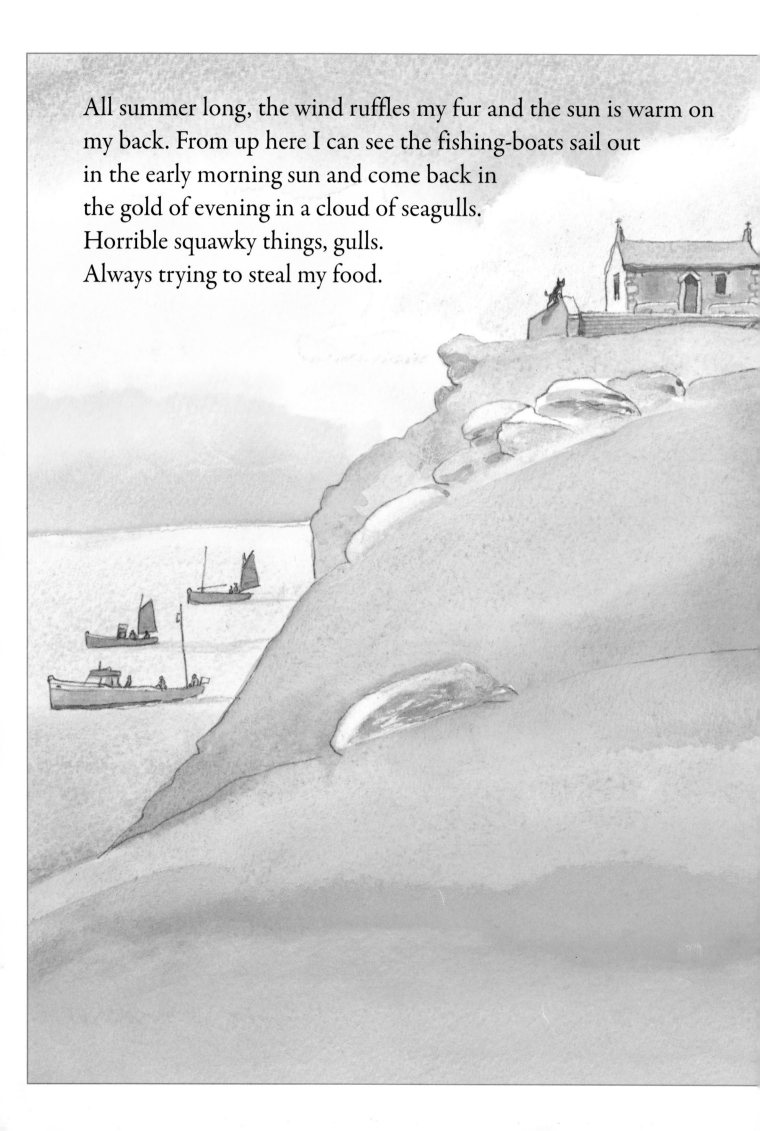

All summer long, the wind ruffles my fur and the sun is warm on
my back. From up here I can see the fishing-boats sail out
in the early morning sun and come back in
the gold of evening in a cloud of seagulls.
Horrible squawky things, gulls.
Always trying to steal my food.

Then, just as the gulls are settling down and I'm ready for a
bit of shut-eye, that damned dog comes racing up the hill,
barking at everything as usual before he runs back down to
the town. Barking mad, I call him.

I'm a ship's cat really, but
I'm slowly getting used
to life ashore.
My old skipper and I used
to come up to this chapel
before we set off on a
voyage. He always said a
little prayer for fair winds
and good weather and then
we would walk down the
hill to the harbour and sail
away into the world.

But my sailing days are over.
The ship and the skipper
grew old together,
too old to sail the seas
and too old to look after me.

# AUTUMN

It's getting cold up here at night now. Trouble is, the days seem to be getting shorter and the cold nights longer. Not many people climb the hill these days, and those who do don't bring ice-cream.

I still see the boats and the gulls and a few surfers still ride the waves. And I can see an old horse and a donkey playing in a field. Must be nice to have a friend. That yappy dog still races past every day. He barks at everything – gulls, waves, clouds, me.

Every evening I go down into the town to look for something to eat.
But I have to watch out. There are lots of town cats around. Rough,
tough, greedy cats who chase me off. I usually find some scraps to
take home for my supper: a piece of pasty at the back of the bakers,
or some dropped chips outside the Take-away. Sometimes the young
fisher boy throws me a mackerel when his dad is not looking.

# WINTER

Brrr. The days are as cold as the nights are now. And wet and windy. When I go out looking for food I get soaked and then can't get dry and can't get warm. Now the horse and the donkey spend most of their time in their stable. I see the man take them out for a trot each day. Then he rubs them dry and gives them a good feed. Lucky beggars!

The weather has been too stormy for the boats to go out so it's been a long time since I had a mackerel. Wet pasty crusts and soggy chips are the best I can hope for. The only good thing is that damned dog doesn't come up here when it's raining.

This evening the little town looks different. There are more stars in the streets than there are in the sky. I can hear singing and I can smell cooking. I think I'll go down and nose around.
I'm starving.

The streets are crowded and the
shops are open, full of light and colour.
I sneak around to the back of the baker's shop.
"Hey, you! Beat it! You don't belong round here!"

It's that fat black Tom with his two ginger mates, Rough and Tough. They're big but I'm quick. I race round the corner and in and out of people's legs, down the street to the Take-away.

No good here, either. More cats. All as
striped as tigers and twice as nasty,
tucking into chips and curry sauce.
People seem to be dropping more
than usual, but the cats won't
share with me – oh no! They spit
at me and show their teeth.

Next I try my luck at the
butcher's shop but the yappy
dog is there. He yaps at me,
and when I run off he chases
after, yapping like a mad thing,
with a string of sausages
round his neck.
Greedy beggar.

I lose him in the crowds and
head up the hill to the safety of
'home'. I'm tired, hungry and
colder than ever.

Snow has begun to fall.

I try to sleep but I'm too cold. Then I
hear that yappy dog. He's coming up the hill!
He *never* comes at night but I can hear him getting
closer and closer.

Now I can see him through the falling snow, and he's
brought some big mates with him. I don't stand a
chance. I back as far as I can under the steps and my
claws are ready.

Then I see he's got a sausage in his mouth. The sausage smells good.

"Hey, Puss, puss . . ."
It's the fisher boy.

"Come on, your friends are here to see you."

Now I can smell fish.
Lovely *cooked* fish.
The horse, the donkey, the dog and the boy are spreading straw on the snow.

"Come on, Puss. Grub's up."

We sit together in the warm straw and eat. It is a feast, and when I can eat no more I climb into the boy's arms. He ruffles and strokes my fur. He is warm on my back.

Bells ding-dong across the bay, and the sea turns silver in the
moonlight. My friends and I sit warm on our hill between
all the stars of Heaven and Earth.

# Other books by Michael Foreman:

9781849392563

9781842705827

9781849393041

9781849390477

9781842704486

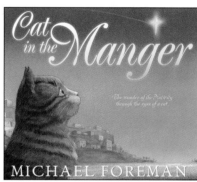

9781842709665